DINO-MIKE

AND THE
MUSEUM MAYHEM

WRITTEN & ILLUSTRATED BY FRANCO

D0928677

Raintree is an imprint of Capstone Global Library Limited,
a company incorporated in England and Wales having its
registered office at 7 Pilgrim Street, London, EC4V 6LB –
Registered company number: 6695582

www.raintree.co.uk
myorders@raintree.co.uk

ISBN 978-1-4062-9396-8 (paperback)
ISBN 978-1-4062-9401-9 (eBook)

18 17 16 15 14 10 9 8 7 6 5 4 3 2 1

British Library Cataloguing in Publication Data
A full catalogue record for this book is available from
the British Library.

Printed in China by Nordica
1214/CA21401920

CONTENTS

Young Michael Evans travels the world with his dino-hunting dad. From the Jurassic Coast in Dorset, to the Liaoning Province in China, young Dino-Mike has been there, *dug* that!

While his dad is dusting fossils, Mike's busy refining his own dino skills – only he's out discovering the real thing. A live T. rex egg! A portal to the Jurassic period!! An undersea dinosaur sanctuary!!!

Prepare yourself for another wild and wacky Dino-Mike adventure, one which nobody will ever believe...

Chapter 1
ON GUARD

"Where do you think you're going?"

Mike looked up to see someone staring at him. He was scowling, his face scrunchy and squeezed like a sponge.

Except he wasn't a sponge. He was a big man with a big moustache. It looked especially hairy, as if someone had placed a broom on his upper lip.

"The museum is closed! You can't go in," the security guard insisted.

"No, no!" a voice from the other end of the corridor shouted. Mike stood on his tip-toes and craned his neck, so he could see over the arm of the guard. "It's okay," continued the voice. "They're with me."

Wearing a white laboratory coat, Dr Giovanni came running down the museum corridor, waving his hand. "They're my guests!" he repeated.

"Sorry, Dr Giovanni," said the guard. "They're not on the list. They can't enter the museum until tomorrow when it reopens."

"Nonsense," said Dr Giovanni. He placed his hands on Mike's shoulder in an almost protective manner. "Don't you know who this is?"

The look on the security guard's face made it obvious that he did not.

"This young man has made the most important dinosaur discovery in the last fifty years!" Mike was convinced at this point that Dr Giovanni was talking about somebody else. "This young man discovered the T. rex eggs that will be displayed this weekend!"

"Really?" The guard squinted, inspecting Mike from head to toe.

"Certainly," Dr Giovanni said. "And this is his father, the renowned palaeontologist Dr Stanley Evans."

Mike's father stepped forwards and shook hands with the guard. "Hello," he said. "Very nice to meet you."

"Obviously, Dr Evans, you've been here before," said Dr Giovanni, "but I believe this is your son's first visit."

"Yes, that's right," answered Mike.

"Well then," began Dr Giovanni as he moved down the corridor and opened a large door. "Let me be the first to welcome you to New York City and the Museum of Natural History!"

Mike and his dad stepped inside.

"Thank you so much for inviting us," Mike said.

"Nonsense! It's the least we can do for our newest and youngest palaeontologist," replied Dr Giovanni.

"Me? A palaeontologist?" Mike asked.

"Of course. You are credited with finding the eggs," Dr Giovanni replied, gesturing towards a glass display case.

There they were – the four eggs Mike had found on his first dino dig. The eggs were roughly the size of cricket balls. He had discovered them on his last Dino-Mike adventure!

On that day, Mike had also discovered a real-life T. rex, a mysterious and possibly time-travelling girl called Shannon, and an evil boy called Jurassic Jeff. Jeff had wanted to release real dinosaurs back into modern-day society.

"Well yes, when you make a discovery such as this," said Dr Giovanni, interrupting Mike's thoughts, "we tend to call you an honorary palaeontologist."

While Dr Giovanni had been talking, the security guard and his moustache had sauntered up to Mike. He leaned in to inspect the eggs more closely. "Where did you say you found these?" he asked.

"On my first dino dig," answered Mike, startled by the guard.

The guard stood up straight and rubbed his chin. "And this was just a few weeks ago?" he asked curiously.

TYRANOSAURUS EGGS

"Yes," said Mike's father. "The other palaeontologists, including myself, missed them. It's lucky Mike was there!"

"Interesting," said the guard, twisting one end of his moustache.

"Yes indeed," agreed Dr Giovanni. "Now let's head to the laboratory to learn a little bit more about them. Mike, if you would like to stay on this floor and have a look around –"

"No, no!" interrupted Mr Broom-moustached Security Guard in a stern voice. "The museum is not officially open. Noboday is allowed in this section at the moment."

"Of course," Dr Giovanni apologized. "I'm sorry, Mike, but rules are rules, and Mr. Broome does have a job to do."

Mike tried not to laugh. He found it funny that the person he had just nicknamed "Broom-moustached Security Guard" was actually called Mr Broome.

"No problem, Doctor," said Mike's dad. "Mike and I can come back and give this whole section the attention it deserves when the museum is open."

"We can certainly give you a discount," offered Security Guard Broome, but it was obvious he wasn't happy about it.

As the conversation between the adults continued, Mike inspected the eggs. Was it his imagination, or were there little cracks on the shells?

Then, as if he were meant to see it, a tiny crack splintered down the egg closest to him. Mike jumped back.

"Is everything all right, son?" asked Mike's dad.

"Yes!" replied Mike.

Mike's dad turned to Dr Giovanni. "Well, let's go and see these fantastic underground facilities."

"Yes!" agreed Mike.

Mike quickly moved away from the display case. As he did, Security Guard Broome eyed him suspiciously.

They left the dinosaur gallery and headed towards a door labelled "Employees Only". Mike trailed behind his father and Dr Giovanni. He reached into his Dino Jacket and pulled out his handheld video game system.

He quickly switched it on.

The message he received from Shannon after his last big adventure flashed up on the screen. But could he respond to it? Mike hoped his message would be received.

He typed, "HELP! FOUND T. REX EGGS! THEY ARE ABOUT TO HATCH!"

"Are you coming?" asked his father.

"Pardon? Oh! Yes! Sorry." Mike smiled and held up his video game. "I was in the middle of a game."

Mike headed towards the stairs with his dad. He glanced back one last time at Security Guard Broome. Broome was glaring at him.

Mike really, really hoped his message would get through to his friend Shannon.

Chapter 2

ALL CRACKED UP

The laboratory was freezing.

Mike was glad he was wearing his Dino Jacket. It was an amazing present from his dad. His dad and a friend had designed the jacket to look exactly as though it was covered in dino scales.

The jacket also had lots of great features that Mike was still discovering.

Mike clicked a button on the inside of the jacket, and three diamond shapes popped out of the back, like the plates on the back of a Stegosaurus. They were actually solar panels and helped heat the inside of his jacket.

"Sorry about the cool temperature in here," said Dr Giovanni.

"Nothing to worry about, Doctor. Your facilities are truly state of the art," said Mike's dad, impressed.

Dr Giovanni was just as excited to have Mike's dad in the facility. "Your findings and research in the field are the reason we are able to do the work we do," he replied.

While the grown-ups talked, Mike couldn't help but worry. What was happening upstairs in the dinosaur gallery? He needed to get a better look at those eggs. You would think that would be easy. After all, they were *his* eggs!

"Oh, Dr Evans, let me show you our newest piece of equipment..." Dr Giovanni said as he ushered them further into the lab.

Mike knew this was his chance to slip away.

Under normal circumstances, Mike would never do anything like this. But these were not normal circumstances.

In fact, since his first dino dig, Mike's life had been anything but normal. Soon after the dig, he had realized that the eggs might belong to the runaway T. rex he and Shannon had captured. Now there were four eggs in the museum about to hatch into four baby Tyrannosaurus rex!

This could be a problem.

A BIG problem!

Mike reached the top of the stairs and peered around the corner at the entrance to the dinosaur gallery. His main obstacle was Mr Broome.

How am I going to get past him? Mike thought.

Mike looked around. *Perfect!*

The security guard desk. That would be his best chance. Sitting behind it was a guard much younger than Security Guard Broome. Not only that, but he seemed to be the opposite of Broome.

Broome was very serious about his job. This security guard did not seem so serious. He sat slumped in his chair with his feet up on the desk.

Mike knew that if he did that at home, his mother would immediately tell him to sit up straight.

The guard was playing with the volume button on his two-way radio while reading a comic book. Mike could use that radio to call Broome away from his post.

Mike stealthily made his way to the desk. He was close enough to grab the radio, but he still had to work out how he was going to get his hands on it.

Mike was crouched down in front of the desk, unseen by the guard, who was more interested in his comic book than anything else. If anyone walked in, they would see Mike immediately.

He had to act quickly!

Mike looked down at his jacket. This was a good time to try out another one of its features. He slowly moved his hands up to the hood's drawstrings.

Mike positioned himself directly in front of a stand that was a couple of metres away and that held pamphlets, maps and information about the museum. He pulled the drawstrings, extending them out with his arms as far as they would go.

As Mike pulled the strings, two streams of water shot from the collar of the jacket like a powerful squirt gun.

SPLOOSH! Direct hit! The stand fell over with a tremendous crash.

The guard jumped up. Mike could see the name Nelson on the man's badge.

Mike moved around the security desk as Nelson came out from behind it to investigate. Mike grabbed the radio Nelson had left on the desk and then quickly made his escape.

Mike made his way back to the dinosaur gallery. Broome was still standing guard, but he was far enough down the corridor that he couldn't see or hear Mike.

Mike turned on the radio and whispered, "Hello."

He heard his voice crackle from Security Guard Broome's radio. Broome pulled his radio from his belt. "Come again, over," he said.

Mike had lowered the volume on his radio so that no one else could hear Broome's voice come through.

He waited.

Broome spoke again. "Nelson? Is that you? How many times have I told you that this radio is not a toy!"

Mike pressed the button and mumbled into the radio.

"Nelson, you haven't handcuffed yourself to your chair again, have you?" he said, waiting for a response.

Mike didn't answer.

Broome barked into his radio as, at last, he walked away from his post. "How many times have I told you that our security equipment is not to be played with! This is the last time I'm going to uncuff you, and this time I'm going to report you."

Mike did not want to see Nelson get into trouble for something he didn't do, but this was important. He ran into the dinosaur gallery and immediately went to the egg display.

He was too late.

The dinosaurs had already hatched!

Chapter 3

RADIO BUTTERFLIES

Four baby T. rex were running around inside the display case. Each one was about the size of a small chicken.

Any minute now the security guards would work out that something wasn't right. They would barge in and find him with four BABY DINOSAURS!

What was Mike going to do?

"Think!" Mike told himself.

Mike reached into his Dino Jacket. He pulled out ... his underwear!

When he was packing for his trip to New York City, his mother made such a big deal about bringing extra clean underwear and socks. He even stuffed extras into the large, hidden pockets of his jacket.

Mike quickly emptied his pockets of all his underwear and then lifted the door of the display case.

He reached carefully for each of the baby dinos and placed them, one at a time, into his jacket pockets.

As soon as they were secured inside his pockets, the dinos began to wiggle, claw and chomp. He was glad that the jacket was made of bite-proof material!

Then Mike quickly squeezed his extra underwear and socks into the broken egg shells, making them look as if they were still whole.

Mike replaced the display glass. If no one got too close, they wouldn't be able to tell the difference. No one would be any the wiser!

"Where do you think you're going?" came the booming voice of Security Guard Broome.

Mike froze in his tracks. He looked down at his overstuffed, wriggling jacket. Then he noticed he was still holding Nelson's radio. He quickly tried to hide it behind his back, but Mike knew Broome must have seen it.

"You are not supposed to be in here! And I'm fairly certain you have something to do with Nelson's missing radio."

"I can explain –" began Mike.

Broome wasn't listening. He was scanning the gallery for anything out of the ordinary. His eyes locked on the egg display case.

Then the guard looked down at Mike's Dino Jacket. Not only was it bigger than last time, but now it was also moving! Broome reached down and grabbed the zipper of Mike's jacket. Mike shut his eyes in anticipation.

Broome opened the jacket.

Four baby T. rex leapt from the open jacket and landed on top of Broome!

Baby T. rex don't weigh much, but the surprise knocked Broome over.

"Ah!" he screamed as he fell down. The four baby dinosaurs scattered in different directions. "D-D-Dinosaurs?!"

"No…" Mike tried to explain, "they're lizards…" In a lower voice he added, "That will grow to tremendous size and be able to eat you in one gulp."

"I was told to expect a possible dinosaur," said Broome, "but *four* baby T. rex?!"

Mike knew it! Broome must have been sent by his enemy Jurassic Jeff! How else could he have known to expect a real dinosaur?

Mike definitely had to get the baby dinosaurs back now. He ran after them.

"Get back here!" shouted Broome as he lunged after Mike.

"Nelson!" Broome screamed over the radio. "He's heading down the corridor towards the Butterfly House."

Sure enough, Mike turned the corner and followed the baby T. rex into the Butterfly House. The T. rex ran through the automatic doors into a hot, sticky, humid room full of plants, trees and butterflies.

Each baby T. rex immediately began snapping at all the colourful butterfly that crossed their paths.

Chomp! Chomp! Chomp!

Once inside, Mike folded down one of the tropical tree branches. He wrapped it around the handles of the automatic doors.

Broome ran in from the other side and smacked right into the doors, expecting them to open automatically.

Getting back up, he tried to manually force the doors open, but Mike had made a good job of securing them.

Mike turned to grab the T. rex. They were still busy snapping unsuccessfully at passing butterflies. He was surprised to see Security Guard Nelson approaching!

"Whoa!" said Nelson. "That little lizard looks just like a real dinosaur!"

Security Guard Nelson dove for the baby T. rex just as Mike noticed a gift shop full of butterfly nets. According to the museum guide, visitors were allowed to catch butterflies with the nets to study them and then release them unharmed.

Mike grabbed one of the nets. Instead of catching butterflies, he used it to catch Nelson! The net flew over Nelson's head and obscured his vision. Then Mike grabbed a second net and used it to catch the T. rex.

Having secured one in the net,
Mike looked around for the other baby
dinosaurs. They were running out of the
door at the opposite end of the Butterfly
House. Mike chased after them before
Nelson and Broome were able to follow.

Mike ran out of the butterfly enclosure and headed back down the corridor towards the dinosaur wing. He knew he was on the third floor. He had to round up the dinosaurs, get down to the ground floor, and get out of the museum without any security guards, any research scientists, or his dad finding out.

That would be the easy part. But what was he going to do with T. rex babies even if he did manage to escape?

"Stop!" came a voice from behind.

Mike froze in his tracks. *So much for not getting caught,* he thought.

Chapter 4

JUPITER SMUPITER

Mike stood as still a statue. The only movement was the squirming of the T. rex inside the butterfly net. If only Shannon had got his message...

"Mike, is that you? It's me. Shannon!"

Mike was shocked. He turned to see his friend. The person he thought, for a split second, that he had imagined.

Shannon was dressed much differently than when he had last seen her. Back then, she was dressed to blend into the forest. Today, she was wearing a shimmery gold top and smart jeans.

"You got my message!" said Mike happily as he greeted her.

Shannon looked confused. "What message?"

Before Mike could answer, Security Guard Nelson appeared behind them.

"Run!" said Mike as he grabbed Shannon by the hand and sprinted down the corridor. Nelson followed, still trying to pull the butterfly net off of his face.

As they raced down the corridor, away from the dinosaur gallery, Mike saw a sign labelled Audubon Gallery.

"Let's try and lose him in the bird section," he said.

"What's going on?" asked Shannon.

Before Mike could answer, Shannon saw a small baby T. rex standing near the stairwell. She stopped and pointed. "What is that?" she asked.

"Another T. rex!" Mike replied.

Mike quickly scooped up the baby T. rex into the butterfly net with the other one. There was only just enough space. He would need something else to put them in.

"Another T. rex?" asked Shannon. "How many are there?"

"You remember our little adventure with the dinosaur we called Sam?" Mike said distractedly as he secured the dinosaur in the net and headed down the stairs towards the second floor.

"How could I forget?" said Shannon.

"Well, after you left, I found four eggs very close to the dig site –"

"OH MY GOSH!" Shannon shouted. "Samantha! The T. rex was a girl!"

They both jumped off the last remaining steps and landed near a sign that read Planetarium.

Signs all over door to the planetarium made it clear it closed for reconstruction. They snuck inside anyway and shut the door behind them.

"Phew!" Mike exclaimed. He slid down onto the floor, slumping against the wall. He pointed to the squirming butterfly net beside him.

"There were four eggs altogether," explained Mike. "They hatched just a little while ago. I captured these two, but there are two more on the loose."

SCREEEEEEEEEEEEEEECH!

Just then, a high-pitched squeal came from above their heads.

Mike and Shannon both looked up. Above them twirled models of the planets in the solar system. On top of the planet Jupiter stood another baby T. rex.

"I think we've just found another one," said Shannon. "I'll climb up and get it."

"Wait," said Mike, grasping his hood's drawstrings. "I have a better idea."

For the second time that day, Mike tugged on his drawstrings, releasing a burst of water. The stream struck the T. rex, blasting it off the planet above.

Thinking quickly, Shannon readied herself beneath the falling dino like a cricket fielder. She grabbed the tiny beast before it hit the ground.

"Good catch!" Mike exclaimed.

"Yes, but now what?" she asked.

Mike looked around. The room was under construction, and he spotted parts of planets scattered on the ground. Some were split into two equal parts, like two halves of a plastic Easter egg.

Mike grabbed two halves of the planet Saturn. He stuck one baby dino inside and then clicked the two halves together. A perfect fit! Mike did the same for the other two dinosaurs they had already caught.

"That should hold them until we track down the last one," Mike said.

Mike and Shannon started walking toward the planetarium exit. "I'm so glad you got my message," added Mike.

"Message? I still don't know what you're talking about," replied Shannon, "I'm here to –"

Just as they reached the exit, the doors suddenly burst open. They both jumped back in surprise.

"I've got you now!" smirked Security Guard Broome.

Chapter 5

DINO FAMILY

"UNCLE RENO!" exclaimed Shannon, leaping into Broome's arm.

"Triceratops?" replied the security guard, surprised to see her.

Triceratops was Shannon's nickname. Only her family called her that. Were Broome and Shannon related?

"You're early!" Broome said.

Shannon finally let him go and said, "I thought I would surprise you!"

"Do you know each other?" Mike asked.

Broome turned to Mike. "You little hooligan!" he said, pointing an accusing finger. "You've got a lot to answer for!"

"Wait, Uncle Reno," said Shannon. "This is my friend Mike."

Broome stopped. "Your friend?"

"Yes," Shannon answered. "This is the friend who helped me capture that T. rex a few weeks ago."

"I thought he might be with Jeff," said Broome.

"Jurassic Jeff?" replied Mike in his own defense. "No way!"

"Then why have you been running all over the museum, stealing radios and causing trouble?" demanded Broome.

"When my dad found out about the eggs, he wanted to bring them here. I had no idea they were going to hatch!" Mike thought for a second and then turned to Shannon. "If you didn't know I was in trouble, then why are you here?"

"My uncle contacted me when the eggs were delivered here," she said.

Broome added, "I heard about the trouble you had with Jeff, so I thought there might be something more to all this ... and it looks as though I was right."

"Well, it's lucky that we're all here to sort out this problem," said Shannon. " Of the four dinos that hatched, Mike has caught three." She pointed to the wiggling planets nearby.

Broome looked at his watch. "We have half an hour before the museum opens," he said.

Broome opened the door to leave the planetarium and came face to face with Security Guard Nelson.

Remnants of the broken butterfly net were still tangled on his head.

"Hey!" exclaimed Nelson. "I've found you! For a second I thought that perhaps the butterflies had gotten the better of you!" Then Nelson pointed to Mike and said, "Isn't that the boy we're looking for, Broome?"

"Yes it is," replied Broome. "Well done, Nelson. Now get back to the desk."

As they all filed past Nelson, Mike handed him back his radio. "I think this belongs to you," he said.

Nelson smiled. "Thanks. I've been looking for this." Then he said, "Hey, by the way, what happened to those little iguanas you were chasing?"

Chapter 6
GONE FISHING

They searched almost everywhere.

"This is the last gallery," said Mike as he pulled open the heavy doors that led to the Oceans of Life gallery.

"What happens if the dino's not in here?" asked Shannon.

"We'll have to think about that when we get to it, but hopefully..."

Mike didn't even have to finish his sentence. The baby T. rex was running backwards and forwards in front of the large aquarium, chasing the fish.

Shannon raised her finger to her lips. The T. rex hadn't spotted them yet. If they kept quiet, they could probably sneak up on it.

SCREEEEEEEEEEEEEEECH!

Suddenly, the T. rex spotted Shannon's glittery T-shirt. It lunged forward, snapping its pointy teeth.

Shannon slowly took a step backwards. But the T. rex took off, running full speed at her.

Shannon sprinted away as fast as she could. She zigged and zagged, leaping over benches and displays, but the T. rex was hot on her trail.

Mike looked up. Among the ocean life displays on the walls and ceiling, he spotted a large fishing net. "I have an idea," he shouted over to Shannon.

Mike scrambled up a nearby flight of stairs to a first-floor mezzanine. He tried reaching for the netting, which was draped across the ceiling above him. It was just out of his grasp.

"Some help would be appreciated!" Shannon shouted as she kept running.

"Hang on!" Mike said.

Without a second thought, Mike stepped onto the mezzanine's handrail. He balanced on the edge of it, six metres above the floor below. A split second later, Mike leapt from the banister and grabbed hold of the netting.

Mike watched Shannon zigzag below him, the baby T. rex still hot on her trail. At just the right moment, he released a set of razor-sharp claws from the cuffs of his jacket. The claws tore through the net, sending Mike towards the floor.

"Look out below!" Mike shouted as he fell with the net.

Ker-pluff!! Mike landed in the gift shop display of dolphin soft toys. The net landed on top of Shannon and the T. rex, trapping them inside.

"Eek!" Shannon screamed.

Mike scrambled out of the toy bin. He helped Shannon out from under the net but kept the dino trapped inside.

"We got it!" Mike exclaimed.

"Yes, we did," replied Shannon. "But the museum is open now. How are we going to get it out of here?"

"I have another idea!" replied Mike.

"Oh no," Shannon sighed.

Chapter 7

BLAST FROM THE PAST

Mike and Shannon stepped out of the Oceans of Life gallery. Masses of museum visitors funnelled into the main entrance. Security Guard Broome ushered them inside.

"I assume everything is under control?" he asked Mike and Shannon.

"Sort of," Shannon replied.

"Where is the..." Security Guard Broome lowered his voice, "T. rex."

Mike held up a large toy dolphin. The toy suddenly jerked in his arms and let out a high-pitched **SQUEEEEEEAK!**

"Is he in there?" asked Broome.

Mike smiled. "We had to think, um, creatively," he explained.

"We'll wait upstairs until the museum closes," added Shannon. "Then we can take all of the dinos to the *Atlantica*."

"That's probably best," Broome said. "I'll meet you upstairs as soon as I can."

Mike and Shannon snuck through the crowd with the undercover dino.

"What's the *Atlantica*?" Mike asked.

"I probably shouldn't have mentioned that," Shannon replied.

"After everything we've been through, you still won't tell me about your secret dinosaur society?" asked Mike, upset.

"I didn't want the information falling into the wrong hands," Shannon replied.

Mike said, "You mean –"

"Jeff," interrupted Shannon.

"Yes, that's what I was going say," replied Mike.

"No," said Shannon, pointing towards the other side of the museum. "It's Jeff!"

Sitting on a bench holding a museum map was the boy responsible for this mess. The boy who set a live T. rex loose on their last adventure. It was his fault that four baby dinos were now running free...

JURASSIC JEFF!

Jeff spotted Mike and Shannon. He gave them an evil glare.

Suddenly, the toy dolphin jerked and fell out of Mike's hands. It flopped and hopped on the floor like a fish out of water. Mike scooped up the toy before anyone could notice – except one person.

Jeff was still staring at them. He gave Mike and Shannon a knowing wink.

"He knows," Mike whispered to Shannon. "We need to get all the dinos out of the museum ... NOW!"

"How?" asked Shannon. "The museum is full of visitors."

Mike grabbed Shannon's arm. "We'll work it out," he reassured her.

The duo made a mad dash for the planetarium. They weaved through the crowd. Jeff was right on their tail.

Mike and Shannon dashed into the planetarium. **Wham!** They slammed the door behind them and held it shut.

"What are we going to do?" asked Shannon.

"I don't know," replied Mike. "It's as though he's been watching us the whole time!"

Just then, Shannon and Mike noticed a man in the middle of the planetarium. He was standing near the model planets that had the other dinosaurs hidden inside them.

Nelson smiled. "Hello, you two," he said, "I found your little iguanas."

Chapter 8

SAY IT, DON'T SPRAY IT

"Two against two," said Jeff as he walked into the planetarium behind them. He stepped towards Mike and Shannon.

"I'm not a cruel person," he said. "I don't want to release these dinos inside the museum. I'd rather do it outside in Central Park. Or better still, in Montana, where I wanted them in first place."

"But why?" Mike asked.

"I'm giving them a second chance at life," said Jeff. "A chance to thrive."

"But think about how much damage this is going to do to our planet," Shannon pleaded. "Don't do it, Jeff."

"You're just scared because you can't stop me!" said Jeff with a smirk.

Mike held up his arms in surrender. "You're right," he said to Jeff. "I don't think we can win."

"Ha!" Jeff laughed. "Look, Shannon, even your friend is giving up!"

Shannon, surprised, stared at Mike. "What are you doing?" she asked.

Then Shannon noticed that Mike was holding the drawstrings of his hoodie.

"THIS!" Mike exclaimed.

Mike pulled the strings again, unleashing his secret weapon. Streams of water shot from his Dino Jacket.

SPA-LOOSH!

The streams blasted Nelson in the face. Mike took the opportunity to grab one of the dino-filled planets away from him. At the same time, Shannon grabbed Nelson's walkie-talkie.

Once Jeff realized what Mike was doing, he rolled the Saturn model away from them and towards the exit. Mike and Shannon followed him.

Shannon pushed a button on the radio. "Uncle Reno!"

"Shannon?" answered his voice. "What are you doing on the radio?"

"Nelson has been working for Jeff!" she told him.

"JEFF?" came the confused response. "How do you know?"

"Because Jeff is here, and he is currently rolling Saturn outside to Central Park," answered Shannon. "I'm following him, and we've just left the planetarium!"

"I'll be there in a second!" said Broome.

Jeff and Mike were rolling the model planets down the corridor. There were more people than before. They stopped and stared at the two young boys rolling planets past them. Although they stopped to look, no one really seemed that interested in what they were doing.

Jeff steered his planet to the top of the stairs. With a push, he tipped it over the edge and watched as it bounced down the stairs. Mike was following closely behind, but then he spotted something. At the end of the corridor, about six metres away from the stairs, the doors to the lift opened.

"This way!" said Mike as he rolled the planet straight into the lift. Seeing Jupiter hurtling towards them, the museum visitors inside the lift quickly leapt to one side or the other. The planet stopped when it bumped the back of the lift. Mike came skidding to a halt, turned to the person closest to the buttons and said, "Ground floor, please."

"We're going down to the ground floor!" exclaimed Shannon as she ran full speed towards the lift.

She only just squeezed through the closing doors. Mike caught her as she fell into his arms.

"Hey," she said, realizing there were other people in the lift with them.

"What's up?" replied Mike.

They both tried to remain calm and not let anyone know that there were dinosaurs inside the Jupiter model.

"Jeff's taken the stairs," said Mike. "I thought this might be quicker."

An old lady with an umbrella next to Mike gave him an odd look.

Mike smiled at her and said, "They're a matching set. The other planet should be downstairs when we get there."

The doors of the lift opened. At that moment, Broome came running up to it.

"Where is he?" asked Broome.

Just then, the planet Saturn came bouncing down the stairs followed directly by Jeff.

"We're going after him!" said Shannon. "The planet and the dolphin in here have the you-know-whats inside."

Broome turned to everyone in the lift and said, "Sorry, everyone, this lift is no longer in service!"

As people filed out, Broome took out his keys and locked the lift door shut with the dinosaurs inside. Mike and Shannon had positioned themselves between Jeff and the exit.

Jeff brought the planet to a rolling halt. He shifted his eyes backwards and forwards across the room.

"It's over Jeff. There's nowhere to go," said Mike.

"He's right," said Broome, moving towards Jeff.

"I don't know about that," said Jeff. "I think I have a few options left."

Mike thought Jeff had no option but to give up. He was wrong.

Jeff reached over to the display next to the bottom of the stairwell. The prehistoric man in the display was holding a crude type of hammer made from a rock strapped to a stick. Jurassic Jeff grabbed the hammer and held it high above his head.

"So much for no options," said Mike.

Before anyone could stop him, Jeff brought the hammer down on the model planet. It broke open into two pieces.

Chapter 9

DINO SCRAMBLE

There was stunned silence on the ground floor of the museum. For a few seconds, no one made a sound. Everyone was staring at one thing.

The baby T. rex had been released from its hiding place. Jurassic Jeff had just unleashed a live dinosaur in the middle of New York City!

The silence was finally broken when the dinosaur opened its mouth and let out a screech. **REEEEEEEEEEE!!**

People in the museum started to run in every direction, shrieking and waving their hands in the air.

Jeff herded the T. rex towards the front door. The tiny T. rex talons clacked on the marble tiled floor.

Mike and Shannon followed behind him. Security Guard Broome went into crowd control mode, so people would not hurt each other.

"I can't believe he's just done that!" said Shannon.

"From what I know about Jeff, I don't think there is anything he wouldn't do!" replied Mike.

By the time they got outside, Mike and Shannon could see Jeff guiding the T. rex across the road. He was even using the pedestrian crossing.

Taxis were honking their horns, and people were moving away from the T. rex. Looking to the other side of the road, Mike saw the trees of Central Park. The giant park was surrounded by concrete in the middle of the city.

"If he makes it to the park, we may never find that T. rex," said Shannon.

Then, an idea from a past adventure hit Mike. "I've got it!" he exclaimed.

On the other side of the road, just in front of the entrance to Central Park, there was a hot dog stall. There were lots of other stall too, selling a range of items from artwork and cheap jewellery to hats and T-shirts for tourists.

"How much money do you have on you?" asked Mike.

"Why? What for?" asked Shannon.

Mike stopped and took all his money out of his pockets and pushed it towards the hot dog seller.

"Oh!" said Shannon, realizing why he needed the money. "You're thinking what mummy T. rex likes, baby T. rex likes!"

"Exactly!" exclaimed Mike.

"Would you like mustard or ketchup?" asked the man selling hot dogs.

"Neither! And you can forget the buns too! I just need the hot dogs – uncooked please!" said Mike.

The man looked at Mike and then shrugged, "I've had stranger requests." He piled twenty hot dogs into a small box and handed them to the duo.

Inside the park gates, Mike and Shannon looked for Jeff and the T. rex. They were close to the forested area of the park.

"He's almost free!" shouted Jeff, laughing at them. "Once he's loose in the park, you'll never find him!"

SPLAT!

"What the –"
was the only thing a
stunned Jeff could say.

After another
second he said, "Did you just hit me in
the head with a hot dog?"

"Yes, sorry about that," said Mike
as he continued to throw hot dogs over
Jeff's head. "I was actually trying to get
that one over you."

Jeff was confused. "Why?"

"Roar!" came a sound from behind.

Jeff turned to see that the tiny T. rex
was snapping up the hot dogs as fast as
Mike could throw them.

Jeff said, "Very funny. But as soon as you run out of hot dogs, he'll leave."

Shannon looked at the box of hot dogs Mike was holding. It was true. Mike was down to half of what he had started with already. Shannon looked down at her T-shirt and then back at the T-shirt stalls just outside the park gates.

"Fine. I'll wait!" said Jeff. "Finish your little feeding frenzy and then watch as this little lizard goes out into the world and grows to full size in the middle of New York City!" Jeff laughed.

"Oh, I don't know about that!" said Shannon, running towards Jeff.

Mike saw her run by and realized she was dressed differently from earlier. She was now wearing an I Love NY T-shirt, with a big red heart on it.

Above her head, she was waving her sparkling, shimmery T-shirt. She looped the gold T-shirt over Jeff's head.

"What's this?" asked Jeff, inspecting the T-shirt that was now around his neck. "This isn't exactly my colour."

"It's not for you," replied Shannon. "It's for him."

They all turned to look at the T. rex. Mike noticed the T. rex was staring at the sparkly T-shirt.

He had seen the same crazed look in its eye when it had chased Shannon around the aquarium.

It thought there was a fish wrapped around Jeff's neck.

The T. rex leapt at Jeff. It knocked him over and pinned him to the ground.

It stood on Jeff's chest and pulled at the T-shirt around his neck with its jaws.

"Ahhhhh! Get it off me! It's going to eat me!" screamed Jeff.

"Only if you promise to stop this crazy plan of yours to repopulate the Earth with dinosaurs!" said Shannon.

Jeff, tired of having his head and chest slammed against the ground, quickly agreed. "Okay! I promise. I will do whatever you want!"

Mike was sceptical. "How do you know he's telling the truth?"

"I don't know," admitted Shannon, "but I don't want him to get eaten either."

"Good point," said Mike. "How do we get it off him?"

Shannon smiled and handed Mike a couple of New York City tourist T-shirts. "I forgot to tell you … I always keep some emergency money in my shoe."

"Nice," said Mike.

"And really," she said, "you should never visit New York City without buying a few souvenirs."

Chapter 10
FILM HERO

Shannon bought three more I Love NY shirts. Two were being used as netting to completely cover and contain the baby dino. The last one Shannon used to tie Jeff's hands behind his back, to make sure he wouldn't try to steal the dinosaur again.

They headed back to the museum.

Mike expected it to be empty or that the police or perhaps even his father would be there. What Mike did not expect was the round of applause that greeted them as they walked in. All the people that were running around scared when the T. rex broke loose from the model planet were now cheering and clapping.

Security Guard Broome came running up to them when he saw them.

"Ha! There you are!" said Broome, talking to the crowd as he gestured to the three of them. "Don't you think they did a splendid job? They had some of you scared, I'm sure!"

The applause got even louder. Broome continued, "Thank you, ladies and gentlemen! Don't forget to see the film at the cinema this summer – Dinosaur Park is going to be a huge box-office hit!"

Shannon guided Jeff through the entrance hall, and Mike struggled against a fidgeting pile of I Love NY T-shirts. When they were well out of earshot from anyone else, Shannon said, "What was all that about, Uncle Reno?"

"Everyone was so panicked when that little T. rex burst out of that ball, so I told them it was a film stunt."

"What?" asked Mike and Jeff at the same time.

"I told them it was a publicity stunt. You know, like something a studio would do to attract attention to their film. They all immediately calmed down."

"So now they don't even believe it's a real dinosaur?" asked Jeff, still not willing to accept what he had just heard from Broome.

"You should be ashamed of yourself! What you did here was a horrible thing! Do you know how many people could have been hurt?" asked Broome.

"It was worth it! Dinosaurs need to roam free just like people do. Don't worry though, I'll make it happen ... one day!" Jeff promised.

"No, you won't!" snapped Shannon. "You've done nothing but cause trouble for weeks now."

"I'm sure you are going to be in BIG trouble when Henry finds out what you've been doing," Security Guard Broome chimed in.

"Henry? Who's Henry?" asked Mike.

Shannon tried to get Broome's attention before it was too late.

"Henry? He's my brother and Shannon and Jeff's father."

It was too late. He had just said what Shannon was trying so desperately to keep from Mike.

"WHAT?" said Mike, this time as an actual question and with a lot more surprise. He turned to Shannon. "Wait, your father? Jeff is your brother?"

Shannon smiled and turned a bright red colour that almost matched her hair.

Jeff also smiled for the first time since they had captured him in the park. "You hadn't told him we're related?" he said.

Shannon was looking at the ground as they walked up the stairs to the planetarium. "No ... but it's not because I didn't want to," she said.

"I'm sorry, Shannon. I didn't know," apologized Security Guard Broome.

"No, it's okay. If anyone deserves to know, it's Mike. He's been so helpful both here and out in Montana. Without him, Jeff would have reintroduced dinosaurs to the world."

"Thanks ... I think," said Mike. "But after everything we've been through together – I can't believe you've never mentioned that Jurassic Jeff is your brother."

By this time, they had arrived at the planetarium entrance.

Jeff decided to speak up. "You think you've stopped me, but you haven't!" he shouted. "I've got friends everywhere!"

"If you're talking about your friend Nelson, I've sacked him. He was escorted by my security team from the premises while you were causing trouble in the park," Security Guard Broome reported.

This bit of news seemed to shut down any other outbursts from Jeff.

"Yes, I thought that might make you quiet," said Broome as he escorted Jeff into the planetarium.

Mike and Shannon remained outside.

"Mike, I wanted…" Shannon began, but Mike cut her off as he handed her the baby dinosaur wrapped in T-shirts.

"It's okay. I understand," said Mike.

Mike put on his best fake smile. "You couldn't even tell me that the bad guy we were chasing was your brother."

"He's been horrible since we..." she stopped herself before she could finish the sentence.

Mike realised she was holding back. "I understand. Dinosaur secrets. Your dad is probably the president of the United States or something." Before Shannon could answer, Mike spoke up again. "Your scary uncle is probably the only one in your family with a normal job ... unless he's a super-secret spy or something."

Shannon laughed. "No, he's a real security guard here at the museum. He has been for almost forty years. It's sort of how my dad became interested in dinosaurs."

She stopped smiling.

There was a long and awkward pause.

"So, I suppose that you and your dad will be looking after the baby T. rex," Mike said finally.

"Yes, we'll make sure they get back to Sam."

"You mean *Samantha*," Mike reminded her.

There was another long pause.

"Well," said Mike. "Speaking of dads, I better go and find mine. He's probably wondering what kind of trouble I've been getting into. But don't worry! I won't tell him anything."

Mike zipped up his Dino Jacket and turned to leave. "See you around," he said to her. Then he turned the corner and headed down the stairs.

He didn't hear Shannon as she waved and said, "Bye."

***

"Hi, Dad," said Mike as he walked into the research facility in the museum's basement. Mike's dad and Dr Giovanni were looking into a large microscope. Papers and microscope slides were spread out across the desk.

"Hello, Mike! Where have you been?"

"Oh, just out and about," replied Mike.

"In the museum? I hope Security Guard Broome hasn't been annoying you too much," said Dr Giovanni.

"No," Mike replied, smiling. "As a matter of fact, he's not so bad after all."

"Really?" said a surprised Dr Giovanni. "He doesn't usually take a liking to that many people."

"I'm sure your jacket was a good conversation point," said his dad, pointing to the Dino Jacket.

"Yes." Mike stroked his jacket sleeve and said, "Trust me dad, the jacket has come in really handy."

"It certainly has," said a deep voice from behind them.

Mike turned to find Security Guard Broom standing at the entrance to the research facility.

"I hope you will forgive the intrusion, Dr Giovanni," Broome said. "But I have a guest who would like to meet Dr Evans, if possible."

Shannon stepped out from behind Security Guard Broome. Mike was surprised to see her.

"Dr Giovanni, I'd like to introduce you to my niece. This is Shannon Broome," continued Security Guard Broome.

"Pleased to meet you," said Dr Giovanni, shaking her hand. "This is Dr Stanley Evans and his son, Mike."

"Hello, Dr Evans," said Shannon as she shook his hand. "I've heard so much about you."

"Have you?" said Mike's dad as he gave Mike a surprised look.

"Yes. I've heard my father talk about you and your research often," replied Shannon.

"Your father?" asked Mike.

Shannon turned to Mike and said, "Yes, perhaps you've heard of him? Dr Henry Broome?"

There was a definite change in the mood of the room. It was very still until Dr Giovanni said, "Reno? Is your brother Henry Broome? Why have you never mentioned this before?"

"Ah, well, you see my brother is..."

"Dad is a very private person. A recluse, if you will," Shannon explained.

"A what?" The question came from Mike before he realized he had even asked it.

"Mike," said his father with a tone that indicated he should not have asked that question.

"No, it's okay. My father doesn't like the spotlight or public places very much. He likes to spend most of his time away from people."

"Dr Broome is one of the world's foremost authorities on dinosaurs. His research is a must-read for anyone going into the field of palaeontology," added his dad.

"Correct," said Shannon. "And when he heard from Uncle Reno that you were coming here to New York City, Dr Evans, he sent me with an invitation. My father would like to know if you would agree to meet him." She turned to Mike and continued, "Of course we would also extend the invitation to your son. My father has heard about his recent discovery of the T. rex eggs."

"Um..." said Mike's father, stunned by the invitation.

"I ... we would like that very much," he finally managed to say. "I've heard rumours that he's living somewhere in Europe."

"Close," replied Shannon, "but more like *Atlantis*."

"Pardon?" asked Mike's dad.

"He lives underwater." Shannon smiled and winked at Mike. "On a submarine in the Atlantic ocean."

Time for another adventure! thought Dino-Mike.

GLOSSARY

Jurassic Period period of time about 200 to 144 million years ago

palaeontologist scientist who studies extinct animals and plants and their fossils

planetarium building with equipment for reproducing the positions and movements of the sun, moon, planets and stars by projecting their images onto a curved ceiling

prehistoric belonging to a time before history was recorded

triceratops large, plant-eating dinosaur with three horns and a fan-shaped collar of bone

tyrannosaurus large, meat-eating dinosaur that walked on its hind legs, also known as a T. rex

DINO FACTS!

Did you know that you can tell the difference between a plant-eating dinosaur and a meat-eating dinosaur by noting how many legs they walked on? Plant-eaters typically stomped around on all four legs. Swift and deadly meat-eaters often hunted on two.

Tyrannosaurus rex had a mouthful of deadly teeth, which were shaped like bananas. But what's the point of those tiny arms? Dino experts think the tiny arms mean that T. rex didn't fight for its food but ate creatures that were already dead. Yuck!

At least one T. rex has left its faeces behind. Scientists examined the fossilized faeces and found bone fragments from a Triceratops in it.

The first fossilized dinosaur eggs ever discovered were found in France in 1869. Today, these eggs remain the largest ever found, weighing more than 6 kilograms and measuring over 30 centimetres long.

What does the word "dinosaur" mean? The word comes from the Greek language and means "terrible lizard." In 1842, palaeontologist Richard Owen was the first person to call dinosaurs by this name.

The world's tallest dinosaur fossil is displayed at Museum für Naturkunde, Berlin's natural history museum. The Brachiosaurus is more than 12 metres high.

ABOUT THE AUTHOR

New York-born author and artist Franco Aureliani has been drawing comics since he could hold a crayon. Currently residing in upstate New York, USA, with his wife, Ivette, and son, Nicolas, he spends most of his days in his Batcave-like studio where he works on comic projects. In 1995, Franco founded Blindwolf Studios, an independent art studio where he and fellow creators can create children's comics. Franco is the creator, artist and author of Weirdsville, L'il Creeps and Eagle All Star, as well as the co-creator and author of Patrick the Wolf Boy.

Franco recently finished work on Superman Family Adventures, and is now co-writing the series The Green Team: Teen Trillionaires and Tiny Titans by DC Comics. When he's not writing and drawing, Franco teaches secondary school art.